kalyug

kalyug

Harsh Vardhan Wig

STERLING

STERLING PUBLISHERS (P) LTD.
Regd. Office: A1/256 Safdarjung Enclave,
New Delhi-110029. Cin: U22110DL1964PTC211907
Phone: +91 82877 98380
e-mail: mail@sterlingpublishers.in
www.sterlingpublishers.in

Kalyug
© 2019, Harsh Vardhan Wig
ISBN 978 93 86245 64 9
With support of Tanvi Jain

All rights are reserved.
No part of this publication may be reproduced, stored in a retrieval system or transmitted, in any form or by any means, mechanical, photocopying, recording or otherwise, without prior written permission of the original publisher.

Printed in India

Printed and Published by Sterling Publishers Pvt. Ltd.,
Plot No. 13, Ecotech-III, Greater Noida - 201306,
Uttar Pradesh, India

The book is dedicated to
the next *Yug*
my daughter
Sara
and
to the little one arriving soon.
A special thanks to my wife
Parakh Wig,
for always being there.

I would also like to thank my parents
Neelima and **Sunil Wig,**
brother **Bharat Wig** and
sister **Sambhavana Wig,**
for their continuous support.

PREFACE

Being a filmmaker the idea for Kalyug first came to me as a film script. Many topnotch production houses were approached for turning the story into a series or a movie; however, even after liking the story, due to commercial reasons, nothing could materialise.

But as this story was very close to my heart, I wanted it to be told and that is when I decided to bring it to the audience in form of a Book.

I decided to pen down the script into a story and while writing I realized how beautiful the process of story-telling is.

I would like to extend my heartfelt thanks to all who have been their and helped me so far in turning my idea into a story. And a special mention and thanks to Tanvi Jain who has acted as a co-author for the book and also Aditya Wig who has lent his support in editing the book.

Harsh Vardhan Wig
harshkyu@hotmail.com

12th August, 2019

CONTENTS

	Preface	7
1.	The Call	11
2.	The Drive	17
3.	The Room	23
4.	Questions And Sandwiches	29
5.	Some Answers, More Questions	37
6.	The Basement	47
7.	Reasons	59
8.	The Incident	69
9.	The Rescue	83

CONTENTS

1. The Call
2.
3.
4.
5.
6. The Rescue
7. Regatta
8. The Incident
9. The Rescue

CHAPTER ONE

THE CALL

Raghav and Mandira was a happy couple.

They were married for six years, and their love had not faded with time. In fact, it had only grown stronger. On their sixth wedding anniversary — on the 17th December — Mandira ordered all of Raghav's favourite dishes: *malai kofta* with *lachha parantha, rajma-chawal* and *rasgullas*. And that evening, as they sat down to eat dinner together, Raghav decided to put aside his favourite habit of watching TV while they ate.

Then, as they relished the last bite of *rasgullas*, Raghav absentmindedly out of his habit picked up the remote and flicked on the news.

Scenes from the Indo-Pakistan border flashed on to the screen, with bright and bold words scrolling at the bottom. The news anchor's tone did nothing to lighten the mood. "Is this another Kargil war?" was the first thing they heard.

Exchanging worried looks Raghav and Mandira, both sat back. Raghav switched the TV off, and the pleasure of the meal began to fade. However, to enjoy the rest of their evening, they took their wine glasses out to the lawn. Raghav put on Mandira's favourite song—*Tum mile, dilkhile, aur jeene ko kya chahiye*—and asked her to dance. They stayed out in the lawn for some time, dancing, singing, reminiscing about the years gone past, looking back to when it was just the two of them, before their daughter Tripti was born.

Sometime around midnight, they decided to call it a night—be it an anniversary or any other day, both had a habit of going to bed on time as they had to get up early for work the next morning.

And then, as they were settling in bed, Raghav's phone rang.

It was his mother, and she sounded upset.

"Beta, beta...", she said and it was clear from her voice that she had been crying for some time.

Raghav sat up straight on his bed, confused yet instantly alert. "What happened, Ma? Are you okay? Is Papa ji okay?"

"Beta, he went for a walk after his dinner, as usual. But it's been more than three hours, and he hasn't returned! The neighbours haven't seen him either! Beta, I'm so worried! It's so cold outside! What if something has happened to him? What if he had an accident? Or someone kidnapped him? He hasn't even called, and he didn't take his phone, and… what if he was…"

Raghav interrupted, "Nothing has happened to him, Ma. Don't worry, I am on my way." He said that while getting out of the bed. "It will only take me a few hours to reach there. If you find out anything, please call me immediately!"

"Okay, beta. Please come fast!"

Mandira, sitting by his side, was watching Raghav worriedly. Then, as he sprang out of bed and dropped the phone, already taking off his T-shirt and walking to the cupboard muttering about his day clothes, she frowned and asked,

"Where are you going? Was that Mummy ji? What did she say?"

"She said that Papa ji went for a walk after dinner but hasn't come back. It's been three hours."

Mandira's frown became deeper and more concerned.

"But Ma…well, you know how easily she gets frightened." Raghav continued. "She sounded properly panicked, and I don't know…I need to go and look for him. Maybe Papa ji stopped at some neighbour's house and just lost track of time—but he hasn't called, and… I need to go. I'm sorry—I'll be home as soon as I can."

Mandira was also out of the bed by then. "Of course, you should go, but…" she sounded worried, "…please be careful!" she said. She walked over to him and wrapped her arms around him. "I'm getting a really bad feeling, Raghav. Should I come too?"

Raghav hugged her back, tightly. "Who'll take care of Tripti?" he smiled, trying to sound normal. "Don't worry, I'll be fine."

With that, he grabbed his car keys, wallet, and was all set to leave.

CHAPTER TWO

THE DRIVE

Raghav was driving for over an hour now. The weather had turned stormy, and since it was winters, at such late hours the roads were mostly empty.

Raghav's parents lived in Amritsar, which was a few hours away from Delhi if one drove very fast. Raghav was in his mid-thirties and was used to both the journey and driving fast. He was puffing on a cigarette as he drove and had turned on the radio to drain out his thoughts, however, it was of no help and he was worriedly chewing his lip when the phone began to ring, and he didn't even hear it for a few times.

Then, as it rang for the fifth time, he picked it up.

"Hi, Mandira."

"What 'Hi'? Where have you reached? I'm

so worried! You could have at least called me after you left to let me know you're okay!" Said Mandira in a worried tone.

"Stop worrying! I'm fine," he said, trying to seem casual.

Mandira's voice abruptly broke, a sob clearly held back. "I don't know why, but I've been... I'm getting really worried. My head feels cloudy since you have left the house—I'm getting scared, Raghav."

"I am absolutely fine, Mandira," he tried again. "Why don't you..."

"There is a *murti* of Krishna on the dashboard of the car, right?" asked Mandira.

Raghav chuckled. "Yes, yes. See, I have God here to protect me. What could happen?"

Just then, the phone line began to crackle. Mandira said something Raghav couldn't hear it, and then the connection began to get even worse.

"Hello? Hello? Raghav can you hear me?"

"Yes, I..."

"Raghav, I can't hear anything, can you…"

The line crackled harder.

"Mandira?"

Frowning, Raghav looked at his phone, and then back at the road. A thick mist had been building for some time, and the road was now draped in a heavy fog. It was almost difficult to drive.

The line went dead.

Raghav called back, but a polite voice informed him that the number could not be reached at that moment and that he should try again later. Despite repeated attempts, he couldn't call home, and Mandira did not seem to be able to call him either. Even calling his parent's home in Amritsar got another polite error message.

Beginning to feel tense, Raghav drove faster. The heavy dinner and many glasses of wine had gone from pleasure to problem — he was sleepy even before eating, and now was yawning frequently as he drove, both worried and exhausted.

Suddenly out of nowhere, a shape appeared in the fog, shadowy, man-shaped and looming directly over the car. The fog was billowing around it, and in the panicked instant that followed, Raghav thought he could see a person standing in the middle of the road, brightly lit by a lamp post but still hidden by the shifting fog.

Then instinct kicked in, and his foot slammed on the brakes as he turned the car, desperate to avoid an accident.

The last thing he heard was the sound of his tyre bursting as it slammed into the divider at over a hundred kilometres an hour.

CHAPTER THREE

THE ROOM

Raghav strained to open his eyes.

His head was pounding, and his whole body ached. As he weakly moved his head, he could feel the dried blood caking the side of his head.

"Wh…" he managed, moving slightly with great difficulty. Everything hurt.

Forcing his eyes open, Raghav blinked blindly, unable to make out anything. He was alone in a room, with a single light bulb shining harshly above his head. He was lying on something, and that was all he knew. That and the pain.

"Where…" he managed this time, his voice weak.

There was no answer.

As the eyes adjusted to the painfully bright light, Raghav could see that he was lying on his back on the floor in the middle of a small, mostly empty room. A large steel door was the only way in or out, and a sealed window high up on one wall.

Raghav passed out again.

When he woke up again, he had no idea how much time had passed. The room was unchanged—but the dried blood on his face had been cleaned away, and there was a faint smell of antiseptic in the air.

Getting up slowly and with great difficulty, Raghav's hands went by instinct to his pockets, looking for his phone. They came up empty.

Looking around, Raghav then noticed a small table next to the door, on which his wallet and phone were lying.

Lurching forward, he picked up his phone, only to find the screen cracked and the battery dead.

'How long have I been here?', he thought.

His mind was hurting almost as much as his body. Raghav began to panic, turning here and there looking for a way out. The door was securely locked, and the sealed window was too high up.

Alternately yanking and pounding on the door, Raghav began to scream for someone to let him out. His voice was weak, and his throat hurt from the accident and from thirst.

The door stayed locked, with no response from the outside at all. Not even knowing if anyone could hear him made it worse. More panicked, Raghav screamed louder and harder, pounding on the door with all his strength.

There was no reply.

No matter how much he shouted or screamed or hit the door, there was no response, no sound from the outside.

Much later, Raghav sat dumbly against a wall, facing the locked door. His body was still aching, and his hands were scraped raw and bleeding from hitting the door. A few tears had come and gone, trickling into his salt-and-pepper beard. Thoughts of Mandira and Tripti and his parents were swarming around his head, and a twisting fear had settled into the pit of his stomach.

Hours later the door was still locked, and at some point, Raghav fell asleep, more tears drying in his beard.

CHAPTER FOUR

QUESTIONS AND SANDWICHES

Raghav was asleep, dreaming about home.

In his dream, he was with Mandira, and they were playing hide-and-seek with their two-years-old daughter, Tripti. Everyone was happy and laughing—and then the dream changed, it became darker. There was a scraping, clicking noise, as though someone was trying to unlock the front door of their home from the outside.

Suddenly, Raghav jerked awake. He was still alone in the empty room, and someone was opening the door.

He crouched back against the wall, suddenly terrified of whoever was on the other side of the door. What if they tried to hurt him?

The door squeaked open slowly, and in the dim light of the corridor beyond, Raghav could see a shadowy shape putting something into its pocket. Then the person stepped forward into the light, and Raghav got his second shock.

It was a woman.

Her hair were tied in a bun, sitting tightly on the nape of her neck. She was dressed in fatigues—whether military or police, Raghav could not tell—and her forearms were heavily muscled. Her eyes were lined with kohl, and a hijab was wrapped around her head.

Raghav stared at the woman dumbly, unable to make sense of what was happening. She said nothing, only stared at him, looking him up and down as though examining a machine that needed a repair. Her eyes were calm but mysterious and there was no sign on her face of what she was thinking.

Raghav's mind was swimming in confusion, and his eyes kept going back to the hijab as though it held the secret of why he was here.

'Why is she…' he thought, before a sharp pang of fear cut through him. The shoulder badges sewn on the woman's uniform caught his attention; they were green and yellow.

"Am I… Are you a Pakistani soldier?" the words spilled out of Raghav's mouth, filled with panic. "You're wearing a hijab, and your uniform is… How could … I don't…"

The woman gave him no reply, and Raghav's panic grew stronger. 'Have the Pakistanis invaded?' the thought was filled with terror, his mind going back to the news report he and Mandira had briefly watched. There was a news of tension at the border, that he knew, but he had assumed it had been further north, near the border. 'Could they have attacked Amritsar? Is that why Papa ji…'

Suddenly overcome with emotion, Raghav got up and glared at the woman.

"Where am I? And who are you? Why have you kept me here, and how long have I been here?" He questioned her without even waiting for answers.

The woman raised a hand, silencing him and gave him a mild smile.

"My name is Sahiba. Major Sahiba. You are safe here."

Raghav continued to glare at her but remained silent.

"Are you hungry?" she asked. "Do you need something to eat or drink?"

As a matter of fact, Raghav was starving. He had no idea what time it was or how long it had been since he last ate, but his stomach rumbled at the thought of food.

The Major nodded to herself and stepped outside the room for a moment.

When she returned, she was carrying a plate with unappetizing looking vegetarian sandwiches and a bottle of water. Carefully putting the sandwiches down on the table near the door, she then tossed the plastic bottle at Raghav.

Catching it as a reflex, Raghav glared at her, then at the bottle. Cracking the seal open, he sniffed at the liquid, and then took a careful sip. It was water, as far as he could tell. He began to drink, and as he tilted his head back, the Major stepped back out of the room and closed the door.

The door squealed as it closed and was locked, and then as Raghav lowered the now-empty bottle, he could hear the Major's footsteps walking away. He was still fearful and angry, but the water had quenched his thirst, and the sandwiches drew all his attention.

Standing up, Raghav walked to the table. His stomach rumbled again, and he began to eat. Despite the fact that the sandwiches were cold and not very good, they tasted like the best meal he'd ever eaten. Soon the plate was empty, and even the crumbs were licked away.

Sitting back down on the floor, Raghav glared tiredly at the door. He was still worried, but the meal had done him good. Nothing made sense — 'How could a Pakistani Soldier be in India? What does she want with me, and... was she even actually a soldier? What the hell is going on?' — and the questions swarming in his mind made him more confused.

Lying down, Raghav tried to make sense of everything that had happened. 'How long have I been here? Where am I?' he wondered, shielding his eyes from the light bulb and staring at the ceiling. 'What... what the hell is going on? Why is a Pakistani soldier...'

Much later, as the questions continued to tumble endlessly through his mind, Raghav fell asleep once more.

CHAPTER
FIVE

SOME ANSWERS, MORE QUESTIONS

Waking up was like fighting his way out of a bad dream, and as Raghav got up, a part of him felt as though he'd just woken into another nightmare.

He was still trapped in the that room, far from his family. God alone knew if his father was okay, or if he'd also been captured, or if he was even alive. And both his mother and Mandira would be worried. How long had it been since he'd last spoken to them? A few hours? Days?

Just then, Raghav heard a loud thud coming from outside the tiny window. It wasn't from inside—of that he was sure.

"Help! Please help!" he shouted suddenly,

hope rising in his heart. "Can anyone hear me? Please help me!"

The thud was not repeated, but Raghav tried again.

"Help! Please, I've been kidnapped! Anyone? Is anyone there?"

Loud footsteps could then be heard from the hallway beyond the steel door. There was the sound of a key grating in the lock, and then the door squealed open.

It was Major Sahiba. She had a grim look on her face.

"Keep quiet!!" she said loudly. "No one is coming to rescue you! Do you hear me? I don't want to hear another word out of you!"

Raghav was struck dumb for a second, but then he found his voice again.

"Somebody please help me! I've been kidnapped!" he shouted as loudly as he could.

The Major was clearly looking displeased.

She stepped forward and grabbed him by the arm, putting a hand over his mouth to stop him from shouting. Raghav was shocked by how strong she was—even with one hand, she could easily hold him still.

"Be quiet," she said softly, looking directly into his eyes. "You're safe here. We're all safe here. If you make too much noise, we'll all be in danger. You have to be quiet, or…" Even though she was speaking softly, the threat was clear in her tone. "I'm going to let you go now. Do you promise not to shout?"

Raghav nodded, and she slowly released him and stepped away.

"Where am I?" he asked. "How long have you kept me locked away in this room?"

"It is the 19th of January," she said. "You were brought here two days ago."

"Why have you brought me here? You're… you're not Indian, are you?"

"No," she said. "You're right about that. I'm from across…"

"I knew it!" he said loudly, backing away.

"What right do you have to be here, to kidnap Indians, and..."

"Be quiet!" she snapped. "If you can't keep your voice down... don't make me do something we'll both regret!"

Raghav fell silent, his mind whirling. "Two days," he said softly. "You've kept me here for two days! My father and mother... and Mandira... I have to..."

"Listen," she said seriously, "you don't understand the situation. I'm telling you, you're safe here. Safer than you would be anywhere else, given what..."

"Are we at war?" he interrupted angrily. "Are India and Pakistan at war? You're going to kill me, aren't you?! Or torture me?! I won't tell you a bloody thing!"

Sahiba stared at him, then shook her head. "Look," she said, "listen carefully to what I'm going to tell you. This will be difficult for you to accept, but I swear to you, it is all true."

"I know what you're going to say. You're

going to tell me that I was driving too close to the Punjab border when the war began, and now because of that, I have been captured, and now you're going to leave me to rot in this prison for the rest of my life!"

Major Sahiba who was clearly trying very hard not to lose her temper, gritted her teeth. "I told you to shut up and listen to me, didn't I? Yes, you're right—we were going to go to war. My unit was near the Amritsar border because we were on high alert. But then… then something else happened."

"What?" demanded Raghav. "What is this 'something else'?"

"There was…. an attack," said Sahiba. "I don't know what else to call it."

"What attack? Who attacked who?"

"We were attacked. We were all attacked. People started dying, suddenly, across the world. No one knows what it is—some sort of chemical weapon or biological agent or something else. But many have already died. Maybe hundreds of millions," she sighed.

"What... I don't... what are you talking about? Who did this?" demanded Raghav.

"We're not sure. We're..."

"And who is this 'we' you keep saying?" Raghav interrupted. "You're Pakistani! This is India! How dare you..."

"Keep your voice down," commanded the Major.

"Who is this 'we'?" demanded Raghav again.

"I told you this would be difficult to believe," said the Major. "Because of this attack... our countries have come together." She shook her head. "The whole world has come together! After the first day... our countries are now allies. Our militaries are working together now, our governments as well."

"What?!" shouted Raghav. "What is this nonsense? Do you think I'm some sort of fool? Stop lying to me! India and Pakistan are working together? What nonsense! Against who?"

Major Sahiba remained silent for a long moment. "Look, if you don't believe what I just told you... this is why we kept you locked away. We didn't know how you were going to react when you woke up, or even what happened to you to make you crash your car. I found your car crashed on the highway, with you unconscious in the driver's seat. You're lucky to be alive and even luckier to be unhurt. Your car was... it's destroyed. Must have flipped at least twice."

"Wait..." Raghav frowned. "The accident... there was someone standing in the middle of the road. It must have been... maybe 1 am or 2 am. Maybe later. The night of the 17th."

"The attack began that night," nodded Major Sahiba. "We started getting reports after midnight. Of people, all across the country, just... going mad, going missing, dying, accidents happening, fires breaking out, bombs going off. Everyone was just... going mad, from shopkeepers to army generals. In my unit, one of my soldiers just started shooting at his own friends. Fifteen people died. Soon after, governments across the world realized this was happening everywhere. That we were being attacked, all of us."

"Who did this?" asked Raghav in disbelief. "What has happened?"

The Major hesitated. "We don't know, but we have an idea," she said. "We know where it's coming from, but we don't know who it is."

"What do you mean?" demanded Raghav. "Stop talking in circles, and just tell me! Who did this?"

Major Sahiba sighed.

"Extra-terrestrials," she said finally. "The earth has been attacked by extra-terrestrials. And for some reason, they decided to land on the subcontinent first."

"What?!"

"Aliens," said the Major. "Aliens attacked the earth. And they're here, in Punjab. Pakistan and India are working together because we have no choice. Because we'll all die if we don't."

CHAPTER SIX

THE BASEMENT

"Do you think I'm an idiot? or may be you think you're a really good liar — but let me tell you, I know a fraud when I see it. You're making all this up. I don't believe you."

"Believe whatever you want to," snapped Major Sahiba in reply to Raghav. "I've told you what I know. And if you can't promise to co-operate — to not shout, to not try and force your way out of the house — I'll have to leave you locked in this room. I can't risk you bringing danger on all of us."

"That's why you're lying," nodded Raghav angrily. "You want me to agree to be locked up! To make myself your prisoner! Or maybe you're trying to make me go mad! This is probably some conspiracy by your government."

The Major was visibly angry, but she only shook her head and said, "Again, you can believe whatever you want to. All I can say is I can't let you leave, because for that I will have to open the door upstairs, and that would allow... whatever is out there... to enter the basement. We all be in danger. We don't even know what's out there right now. For all we know, the aliens have now actually landed, and..."

"There are no aliens," said Raghav loudly. "You're lying."

"...and so we can't open the upstairs door," Major Sahiba finished her sentence. "I don't care what you believe. If you promise to cooperate, you can come out of this room, into the basement with us. If not, you can stay in this room forever, for all I care."

Raghav was angry, but he wanted to leave the room. And even though he didn't believe the story he'd just been told, he could see that Major Sahiba was telling it as though she believed it to be true. Either she was a fantastic liar, or it had actually happened.

"Aliens attacking earth," Raghav muttered to himself. "What rubbish." Then, he sighed. "Whose house is this anyway? Isn't it yours?"

"No, it isn't. I'll tell you everything once you will promise to cooperate."

Raghav was silent for a long moment. "Can I have some food? I'm really hungry," he then said.

Sahiba nodded, "We have food, but not a lot. If you'll promise, you can come out. Look, I need you to cooperate, not to believe me. And I won't ask you to do anything except for not trying to leave the basement. That's it."

Raghav shook his head. "Do I have an option, Major?"

Sahiba nodded, and then led Raghav out of the small room and into the larger basement beyond.

Raghav's eyes widened as he walked out of the little room he'd been locked into. The basement walls were lined with shelves that were stacked with hundreds and hundreds of books. There was a small kitchen in one corner, with a fridge standing nearby, with a four-seater dining table next to it. Another door led into a dingy looking washroom. The other side of the basement had two sofa-chairs facing a longer sofa. And an old man — somewhere in his sixties — was lying on the larger sofa, either asleep or unconscious. Beyond the sofa was a staircase leading to the ground floor of the house.

Sahiba went to the fridge and opened it. Looking over her shoulder, Raghav could see that there was very little food inside, and only a few bottles of water.

"Will you now tell me where are we — whose house is this? And if it isn't yours, how did you come here? And who's that old man lying on the sofa?"

Sahiba turned away from the fridge and put a bowl of salad and a fork down on the table. Gesturing for him to take a seat, she sat down too and said, "one question at a time, please."

"Fine. How did you come here? And how did I come here?" He picked up the fork and took a bite of the salad.

Sahiba shook her head.

"My team, like I told you, was near Amritsar, at the border. Two nights ago, we started getting reports of… people going crazy. We thought it was an attack by the Indian side—our HQ thought it was some sort of chemical weapon—so we were ordered to advance. Around 3am we crossed the border. A little while later—when we had reached the highway, I found your car—there was a bright white light in the sky, and this loud bang. Like some enormous missile had gone off somewhere, except there was no missile in the sky. Just the light."

Raghav, looked at her in extreme disbelief, said nothing, and continued eating.

"Anyway," Sahiba continued, "the light became so bright that I couldn't see anything. Then I lost consciousness. When I woke up… I was the only one of my team who woke up, rest were dead."

Raghav stopped eating, and stared at the Major. She spoke as though she believed every word she was saying, but what she was saying was... almost impossible to believe.

"When I got up... my radio wasn't working. It might have been an EMP blast, that white light... it knocked out all the radios my team was carrying. All our electronic equipment. I managed to get one radio working, though, for just long enough to get a message from my HQ. They told me what I told you — that the attack was not from anyone on earth, that it came from outer space. That world governments were now working together. And that the... chemical attack, or whatever it was, had gotten worse. I was told to find a safe place, underground, and to wait for the soldiers."

"What soldiers?" demanded Raghav. "Pakistani soldiers?"

"You're not listening," snapped the Major, "we're all working together now. That's what the message from HQ was. That all the armies on the subcontinent — all the armies on Earth! — are working together. I don't know which soldiers are going to come to rescue us. They might be Indians, for all I know. But they will come. And we can't leave this basement—that door upstairs will not be opened—until they arrive."

"How did I get here?" asked Raghav, beginning to feel uncomfortable. Having eaten most of the salad already, his hunger had disappeared, taking his anger with it.

Major Sahiba's story was entirely unbelievable, yet she told it as though it was entirely true. And more importantly, Raghav knew both how strong she was, as well as the fact that there was a gun holstered at her hip. She had stared very directly at him when saying that the basement door would not open until their rescuers arrived, and had put her hand on the gun for emphasis.

"Like I said, we had made it to the highway when we saw the flash of light. I was the only one of my team who woke up, and after I radioed HQ, I started walking along the highway, looking for somewhere to take shelter. I saw your car, crashed on the side of the road—you were inside, unconscious.

I pulled you out, and carried you until I found this house. It's the only one on this part of the highway — the owner must really like to be alone."

"Is that him?" Raghav nodded toward the man lying on the sofa.

She nodded. "I found him like that, upstairs, when we arrived here. I dragged both of you down here. He has woken up twice since, but he falls asleep soon after. I think the chemical in the air has affected him. He just nodded when I told him my story the first time. I was hoping that may be he was not affected as he was inside a house when it happened. Also, because this is a very isolated stretch, quite far from urban areas."

"How were you protected? Why didn't you become unconscious?"

Sahiba shrugged, "I don't know, HQ said that the attack didn't affect everyone — most of them, but not everyone. Some people went mad right away. Others just fell asleep, but that was even worse. Pilots fell asleep. All over the world. Train and bus drivers too.

The number of people who died in... in 'accidents', in just the first few hours..."

Raghav shook his head. "This... this is a lot to take in. But..." his mind whirled, trying to find some way to make sense of it all. "Why did you bring us into this basement? Wouldn't it have been easier to lock the doors of the house and just stay upstairs?"

"I don't know how dangerous that could be," she replied. "The basement is easier to seal off from the outside. There's more chance of escaping whatever's in the air if we stay down here. And help should be here soon."

Their conversation was interrupted by a loud cough from the sofa.

Both Sahiba and Raghav swung around, just in time to see the elderly man sitting upright and rubbing his eyes. Getting up, he smiled at them and then walked slowly to the table.

"What the hell is going on?" muttered Raghav to himself as the old man sat at the table, nodding to Sahiba as though they had met before.

"Hell is exactly what is going on," the old man said then, as though answering Raghav's question. "And of course, it had to happen, didn't it? Everyone knows."

CHAPTER SEVEN

REASONS

Professor Pandey — that was what Sahiba called the old man — looked like a stereotypical hippie. He had a locket on a chain around his neck and was wearing a Rudraksha earring in one ear. He had a heavy beard and thinning hair, both of which were going to white.

The three of them sat in awkward silence for some time, before Raghav spoke. "What did you mean 'this had to happen'?"

"Before I answer you," said the professor, "If I can ask, who are you? I know Major Sahiba — at least, I met her yesterday, when she rescued me from upstairs — but who are you?"

It was Sahiba who answered. "He's the person I told you about, professor. He had an accident, and I found him unconscious on the highway. I didn't know if he had been poisoned by whatever is in the air, so I had locked him in the other room until he woke up. He knows everything I told you. He's agreed to cooperate."

"Cooperate?" questioned professor Pandey.

"He's not going to try to open the upstairs door until help gets here," answered Sahiba.

Uncomfortably, Raghav interrupted. "Now that you know my story, would you please tell us what you meant by saying 'this had to happen'? You believe Major Sahiba's stories about an alien attack?"

"Yes," smiled the professor. "But she's only partially right."

"What do you mean by 'partially'?" Raghav's voice had a tinge of irritation.

"I believe we've been attacked by something from beyond Earth. But I don't think 'alien' is the right word to describe them... to describe it."

"So what should we call it, then? An act of God?"

"Maybe."

Even Sahiba couldn't contain her surprise.

"With all due respect, professor, what you're saying... I mean... what are you really saying? Allah, coming to destroy mankind? Surely you realize... that sounds absurd!"

Just then the professor got up, and started searching a cabinet near the fridge. "Here we are," he said to himself. There was a clinking sound, and he brought a half-bottle of whiskey out of the cabinet, along with three glasses. Setting them down on the table, he handed the bottle to Raghav. "If we're trapped down here, this should help pass the time. And," he turned to Sahiba, "if you're actually interested, this story might take a while."

Then, as Raghav and Sahiba continued to stare at him, he gestured at the bottle. "Pour us all a drink, will you?"

The Major refused her glass, but soon Raghav and the professor were both settling back with a glass in hand.

Raghav nodded to the professor. "Thank you for the drink—but now, if you'd please explain what you said earlier...?"

The old man suddenly became serious, as though he were a lecturer preparing to teach his students a thing or two. He had a slow way of talking, explaining things that most people already knew, but both Raghav and Sahiba let him talk.

"First, let me tell you a little about Indian history. According to Hindu mythology, there are 10 avatars of Lord Vishnu that will appear on the Earth. Nine of them—namely, Matsya, Kurma, Varaha, Narasimha, Vamana, Parashurama, Rama, Krishna and Buddha—have already made their entrances in the different Yugas. That is, they appeared and did what they were meant to do in the Sat Yuga, the Treta Yuga and the Dwapar Yuga. Now as per our ancient texts and writings, only the 10th avatar is yet to be seen."

Holding his glass, the professor stood up and walked slowly to one of the many shelves bolted to the basement walls.

"Now, only the 10th avatar, Kalki—which, according to our texts is supposed to make its presence known to the humankind in the Kal Yuga—remains to be seen."

Picking through a few books, he selected one and brought it back to the table. It was heavy, printed on glossy paper, and had a one-word title—Prophecies. It turned out to be filled with pictures of ancient manuscripts, with long passages of translations in Hindi and English.

"And as you may know," the professor continued, going back to the shelf, "many believe that we are living through the Kal Yuga at this very time."

Raghav was quiet. He didn't believe a word of what the professor was saying. Even the Major's explanation of an alien invasion was more believable. And at any rate, he didn't believe that either. But she had a gun, and he had no way of knowing what was going on outside the basement. 'Papa ji', he suddenly thought with a sharp pang of worry. 'It's already been two days. Who knows what could have happened by now...'

Pushing aside his worries about his parents and Mandira, Raghav tried to pay attention to the professor, who had continued his lecture.

"...when humans have destroyed the Earth with their lusts and habits and atrocities, Kalki will appear. Our ancient texts say that a time will come when our world is plagued by corruption, greed and ill-will. Murder and theft become everyday events, and even heinous crimes like rape become commonplace. The rich become cruel, and ordinary people find it difficult even to breathe. Life becomes a chase for money. Humanity is forgotten and even families fall part, fighting for money and status and power. Children forget their parents, and all dharma is lost. And, our scriptures say, that is when Kalki will appear and guide humanity back onto the path of righteousness..."

Raghav glanced at Sahiba. She had an openly disbelieving look on her face, as though she was only just tolerating the old man's nonsense. Raghav felt a sudden surge of anger — what right did a Pakistani officer, one who had kidnapped two Indians, what right did she have to judge anyone? It was because of her that...

"...tell me," the professor said loudly, "what day is it today?"

Raghav looked up in surprise. The professor had collected a few more books from his library, and was bringing them back to the table.

"Uh... Thursday," said Raghav, just as Sahiba said "The 19th, professor."

Nodding, the professor opened one of the books he'd brought to the table to a specific page, and offered it to Raghav and Sahiba. "There, see the translation."

"The avatar will appear on a white horse, and will cleanse the world of sin," Sahiba read aloud. "He will scourge the world with fire, and only the righteous will survive.

And it will begin on the 17th day of the first month..."

Raghav could not contain his disbelief. It came out in a shout of laughter.

"So God himself has come to save us from our lewd politicians and rapists and thieves?" Despite the injured look on professor Pandey's face, Raghav continued to laugh. "I'm sorry professor, that's the most ridiculous thing I've heard, and that's including Major Sahiba's story about an alien attack. All we have to do is step out of this basement, and you'll see that..."

"Nobody is going upstairs," snapped Sahiba. "Not until help arrives."

"And how will we know when that is?" demanded Raghav suddenly. The whiskey had made him brave, and for a moment, the gun on Sahiba's hip was a less painful idea than not knowing if his family was safe. "How exactly will we know when your 'help' has arrived, Major Sahiba? What if you're lying, and it's just the Pakistani army, huh? For all we know, war broke out between

India and Pakistan, and you're just lying so that we'll help you hide here until your reinforcements come. Why shouldn't we…"

"I'm not lying," Sahiba said angrily. "I could have shot you whenever I wanted over the last two days. I didn't even have to rescue you from your car, I could have just left you to die. I'm not lying about the chemicals in the air. It's too dangerous to go upstairs."

"Don't fight, don't fight," the professor mumbled just then. He then picked up the bottle of whiskey again, and started refilling his and Raghav's glass. "Here, see these books. Read this, you'll see there's nothing to worry about. This was all foretold."

Raghav and Sahiba looked away from each other.

Raghav was still determined to get out of the basement, but the look on Sahiba's face had made it clear she was ready to shoot him if necessary. He shook his head, turning to the professor to hide his anger.

"Ok professor," he said. "Tell me more. Do we know anything else about Kalki?"

CHAPTER EIGHT

THE INCIDENT

Over the next few hours, the professor gave Raghav and Sahiba more of a lecture than they might have wanted. Neither interrupted, however, both sitting in stony silence, listening as he babbled on and on about mythology and history and what revelations were being found as ancient documents continued to be deciphered.

Raghav was hoping that Sahiba would eventually drop her guard and go to sleep so that he could steal her gun. However, she had not had even a sip of the whiskey and seemed more alert than he did. For her part, Sahiba seemed to be waiting for him to fall asleep so that she could relax — every so often, Raghav would catch her staring at him and frowning, as though regretting saving his life.

And so, for the next few hours, they were given a detailed lecture on everything Pandey knew about the topic mixed in with many of his beliefs and opinions.

"And this is the truth! After all that the planet has endured, God has to come to rid us of our sins. You can call him an alien or an avatar or God—that doesn't change the fact that God is finally here. I can feel it; yes, I can feel him! He is here, riding on a white horse through the streets of this world, a world that we have defiled by our..."

Eventually, the professor grew tired of talking, and lay down on the sofa again. Soon, he dozed off, snoring contentedly. He had finished most of the whiskey himself and was the only one in good spirits. Raghav and Sahiba continued to sit at the table, not trusting the other enough to fall asleep.

Sahiba eventually picked up a book and began to read. For a lack of anything else to do, Raghav got up and started wandering around the room, reading the titles of the hundreds of books the professor had collected. Most were historical in nature, with many books of maps and translations and photographs of ancient sites. There were a number of conspiracy-theory compilations as well, some about ancient aliens, others about hidden underground cities and secret societies that controlled the world. One entire bookshelf seemed dedicated to books about one specific ancient temple in India.

Eventually, Sahiba relaxed a little, becoming interested in something she was reading. She had put her feet up on another chair and was frowning at the book, all her attention clearly on it. More importantly, her back was to the basement, to the staircase leading upstairs.

Raghav was drunk a bit as well and was feeling bold enough to take a few risks. Carefully, he tiptoed his way up the staircase to get a look at the door. It was a strong steel door, like the one he'd been locked behind, and it was padlocked with a heavy, rusty old lock. Sahiba probably had the key, Raghav thought bitterly. Impossible to break without a crowbar or a hammer and a chisel, and there was no way that could happen quietly enough for Sahiba not to interfere before he managed to escape.

'And what if she's not lying?' the thought came to Raghav suddenly. 'What if she's telling the truth?'

Feeling uneasy, Raghav tiptoed back down the staircase. By the time Sahiba turned to check on him again, was pretending to browse another bookshelf.

About half an hour later, Raghav sighed tiredly and admitted defeat.

Sahiba still looked as alert as ever and had even finished the book she was reading. She had started on another, after offering Raghav more sandwiches and eating a few herself. The professor was still asleep.

'I might as well sleep too,' thought Raghav tiredly, sitting down on one of the sofas. 'Maybe I'll think of something when I wake up. God, please let everyone be okay.'

Raghav woke with a start.

He dreamt of Mandira and Tripti again, and his mother's phone call. The accident that led him here—the looming shape in the fog that made him lose control of the car—were part of the dream too.

The basement was exactly as it was when he fell asleep—Pandey was still snoring on the largest sofa, and Sahiba seemed to be still reading, seated at the kitchen table some distance away. It was impossible to tell how much time had passed. There were no windows in the basement.

"Major," said Raghav stretching his arms and yawning, "what time is it?"

There was no reply.

"Major?"

There was still no reply.

Turning around in surprise—Raghav stared at her. She was still seated at the kitchen table in front of a pile of books, with her back to the rest of the basement. Her feet were up on another chair, but she was sitting upright.

Raghav rose to his feet as silently as he could, his heart began to hammer. 'Maybe she's asleep,' he thought excitedly, the adrenaline chasing away his own tiredness. He turned this way and that, craning his neck to get a better look at the Major, but all he could see was her back. She had still not responded, or given any indication that she heard his question.

'Okay, I can't make a sound,' Raghav thought to himself.

He'd been dreaming about escaping since he'd woken up, and in the back of his mind, was still frantically worried about his family. 'If she wakes up, there's no way I'll ever get out… and I could even get shot.'

Walking slowly, Raghav stepped away from the sofa, measuring the distance to the kitchen table. It was only four or five steps to where Sahiba was sitting. The Major still had her feet up, but if there was a book in her lap, Raghav could not see it. Her head was up, though—not drooped forward as though she had fallen asleep while reading.

And on the table in front of her, within easy reach, was Sahiba's holstered revolver.

For a moment, Raghav just stood there, wondering what do to. Should he just rush forward and grab the gun? If she were awake, she'd hear his first step, and that would be it. He'd never reach in time. But what if went slow and tried to be quiet? That would give her more time to hear him, and if she woke up, there would never be another chance as good as this one.

And then, while Raghav stood silently, staring at the gun and arguing with himself in his mind, there was a loud thump from outside the basement.

And then another.

Sahiba's feet slipped off the chair suddenly, and her head jerked in surprise as though she'd suddenly woken up.

Raghav cursed softly as she began to turn—and then there was another, even louder thump from outside the basement. Almost, in fact, as though it had come from right outside the basement.

Sahiba stood up quickly and turned to find Raghav staring at her from across the basement, his eyes filled with worry. "What was that noise?" she said, taking a few steps toward the staircase. "Did you hear that as well?"

'She doesn't know,' thought Raghav excitedly, struggling to keep his face blank. Sahiba's eyes were still unfocussed from sleep, and it seemed that she'd forgotten that her gun was on the table, not at her hip.

"Did you hear…" she asked again, turning to look at the staircase.

Raghav began to run.

Sahiba turned in surprise at the first thudding footstep he took, but almost instantly realised what was happening. Her hand went to her hip, where her gun should have been, and she began to run as well.

But Raghav was quicker.

Reaching the table, he snatched up the gun and almost tore it out of the holster, his hands trembling from the adrenaline. Pointing it at her with both hands, he stepped backward, away from Sahiba.

"Stay back!" he shouted. "Stay back, Major, or I'll shoot you!"

Sahiba had reached the kitchen table as well, but had stopped, freezing in place. "Be very careful, please," she said seriously. "Have you handled a gun before? It could go off accidentally."

"Shut up!" shouted Raghav, his hands still trembling. "And stay back!"

Sahiba took a step backwards, raising her hands to show she was not trying to threaten him. "Okay, okay. I'm moving away. Please, be careful, that is loaded…"

"I need to leave," said Raghav suddenly, interrupting Sahiba.

On the other side of the basement, professor Pandey was waking up as well, coughing as he did. "What's all that noise?" he asked, coming awake and rubbing his eyes. "Who's shouting?"

"I need to leave," Raghav said louder, staring directly at Sahiba. "Please unlock the door, Major. I need to find my family. I need to get out of this basement!"

"If I open the door, we will all be in a lot of danger," said Sahiba softly. "I can't do that. My orders…"

"Damn your orders!" shouted Raghav, his anger flaring up again. He was hungry and thirsty and worried, and the whiskey had left a foul taste in his mouth. "I need to get out of here, do you hear me? Damn your aliens and your prophecies, damn both of you liars! I'm leaving right now! Open the door, Major, or I'll shoot you!"

"I can't do that…" she began again, and Raghav squeezed the trigger.

In the enclosed room, the sound of the gunshot was shockingly loud. Raghav's hands jerked backward and he almost lost hold of the gun as it recoiled. His hands had been trembling anyway, and he had been aiming upward—he had intended to frighten Sahiba, not to actually shoot her.

Some distance away, the Major was staring at him in shock and anger from behind the sofa. She'd been incredibly quick, taking cover as soon as the gun had fired. Behind her, professor Pandey also looked stunned.

There was a bullet hole in the wall behind Pandey, and the acrid smell of burned gunpowder in the air.

Then, before anyone could speak, the thudding noise from outside the basement resumed. Again and again and again the thudding came, louder and louder as though now coming from the floor right above them.

"What's... what's that sound?" asked Raghav in fear, pointing the gun at the staircase. "Major? Are those your friends upstairs? What's going on?"

"I don't know," she replied, backing away from the staircase. "And if you have any sense, you'd give me my gun right now. You don't know how to use it, and..."

"They are here!" shouted Pandey then, in excitement. "The lords, they have come!"

"Shut up!" both Sahiba and Raghav shouted at the professor.

And just then, the thumping went silent.

Raghav realised suddenly that he was sweating—big, salty droplets that burned his eyes and made his hands slippery—and that his hands, pointing the gun at the staircase, were trembling as though he had a high fever. Some distance away, Sahiba was dividing her angry glares between the staircase and the gun, and beyond her, Pandey was staring directly at the ceiling with his eyes shut, lips moving in silence as though he was praying.

There was a long moment of silence.

And then, the door leading upstairs exploded out of its frame with a shattering sound of twisting metal and gout of red flame. As the smashed pieces of metal came tumbling down the staircase, a choking cloud of grey smoke followed. A moment later, the grey haze pouring into the basement was filled with bright spots of light that moved this way and that.

"Drop the gun!" someone shouted. "Drop it now, or we will shoot!"

"What?" shouted Raghav, staring at the figures that were becoming visible in the grey haze. People were coming into the basement, many people, all of them wearing futuristic-looking gas masks and carrying assault rifles with torches strapped to them.

There were two loud cracks, one after another, and Raghav found the gun spinning away from his hand as his left arm went numb. He slammed backwards into the wall, only then noticing that he seemed to be bleeding out of his shoulder.

"Major?" Raghav could hear one of the figures saying to Sahiba. "Major Sahiba, I presume?"

CHAPTER NINE

THE RESCUE

Sometime later, Raghav regained consciousness.

He was outside the house, lying on his back in the lawn. Someone had put a gas mask on his face, and two people were winding a bandage around his shoulder.

"...a clean through-and-through shot," one of them was saying to the other. Both were wearing army fatigues and body armour, but they also had big red crosses painted across their chest-pieces. "Good thing we didn't have to cut the bullet out. He'll be fine in a few days."

Then, as Raghav blinked his eyes in the painful light, "Oh look, he's waking up."

The sky was grey and overcast, even more than it should have been on a winter's day. It was cold, much colder than Raghav remembered it being only a few days ago, and the world seemed quiet. There was no distant sound of traffic, and even the animals and birds seemed to have gone silent.

As the two medics helped Raghav to his feet, he looked around to get his bearings. He recognized where he was almost immediately—barely half a kilometre from where he'd had his accident—on a desolate part of the Amritsar highway. He'd frequently passed this place on his way to and from his parent's house. It was a short stretch—only five or seven kilometres long—through a very undeveloped area. There was nothing here except empty land and professor Pandey's solitary house.

Raghav could see the army vehicles that were parked on the side of the road—an ambulance and an army transport vehicle among them—as well as a number of outrider jeeps, all fitted with radios and armour. A group of commandos was clustered around the vehicles. They were wearing a number of different kinds of uniform, but all were armoured, and wore gas masks, and all of them were carrying assault rifles.

As Raghav came to his feet, three uniformed soldiers approached him. Raghav recognized one of them from the basement — it was the first man to come down the stairs, the one who had been shouting at him to put down the gun. Then, with a shock, Raghav recognised Major Sahiba as well — she was following that man, and was also wearing body armour and carrying a rifle.

"Your name is Raghav?" demanded the first man. "Major Sahiba says that's your name. Correct? Quickly, now, we don't have much time. We have to leave quickly."

"Yes," said Raghav, with his worries returning. It was unbelievable that Sahiba had been telling the truth, but there it was. Soldiers had come to rescue them, and from this man's uniform, he was with the Indian army.

"She's told you the situation? Do you have any questions?"

"Who are you?" asked Raghav.

"Captain Arjun, Indian special forces. That's all you need to know. We'll be escorting you to our base, and we'll see about getting you to a refugee camp after that."

"Refugee camp?" asked Raghav, his fear grew. "What the hell do you mean? I need to go home! And check on my parents! I was going to Amritsar to…"

"It doesn't matter," interrupted the Captain. "You can't go to Amritsar. Maybe we can put you on a bus to Delhi. We'll have to see. Most transport has been seized by the Army. We've got a lot of work to do. It's not easy coordinating so many different armies."

"What the hell are you talking about, Captain?" shouted Raghav in panic.

Just then, another medic appeared out of the crowd of soldiers, with professor Pandey in tow. He was also wearing a gas mask, and looked even crazier than before.

"I tried to explain the situation to them earlier Captain," said Major Sahiba. "Clearly, they didn't trust a Pakistani."

The Captain frowned irritably, then shook his head. "Listen, both of you," he said to

Raghav and professor Pandey, "Major Sahiba was telling the truth. We don't know who it is, or why it's happening, but this—", he waved an arm at the grey sky, " — this didn't come from this planet. Satellites picked it up coming from beyond the Earth a few days ago, before the attack started. I don't know if it's God or if it's an alien force—but there is something in the air that is... that makes most people fall unconscious. We're trying to rescue whoever we can, but so many have already disappeared, from so many places..."

"Yes!" Raghav interrupted. "That's what happened to me! My father also disappeared! I was driving to Amritsar to go search for him!"

"Yes, we've recorded a lot of missing person cases. But that's just a small part of the madness. The earth itself seems to be going mad. There have been some terrible earthquakes across the Indian subcontinent. People are dying, and nobody knows where these disasters are coming from. In Chennai, when the attack began, a bright white light filled the entire sky, and anybody who saw it turned blind instantaneously."

Raghav was silent, as was Pandey. The story was unbelievable, but so was the fact that an Indian army Captain had rescued them, just as the Pakistani Major had said would happen.

The captain must have picked up on Raghav's disbelieving glances at Sahiba.

"Yes," he said. "All the countries across the region are working together. We have soldiers from Pakistan on our team. There are army officials from China leading soldiers from Bangladesh. I have Sri Lankan special forces soldiers under my own command. There are no borders at this point."

"What the hell is going on?" mumbled Raghav. His shoulder was beginning to ache.

"Nobody really knows," shrugged the Captain, leading them toward a military transport. "You don't know how bad it is in the cities. People are lying on the streets, in the open, unconscious. Tens of thousands of them. We want to help them, but we don't know what to do. They don't respond to any treatment. They just lie there, unconscious. HQ thinks it's some sort of virus. So, our job is to rescue the people who escaped, who may be immune, and to take them to safety." He shook his head. "People make up all kinds of stories when they're scared. All we really know is that this attack… it came from beyond the earth."

Then, as nobody replied, the Captain continued. "As I said, we don't have much time. We need to get you to safety, and to rescue others in the area. We've wasted a lot of time here. Now, if you'll please cooperate, I would be in a position to save your lives, as well as the lives of those like you who have absolutely no idea what's happening."

Arriving at the truck, they were made to sit in the back with a number of other soldiers and refugees. Many of the other people who had been rescued looked as frightened and confused as Raghav felt, and there was a pitifully small number of them.

Soon, the military convoy was on its way, barreling down the highway at full speed. Armoured jeeps were flanking and leading the convoy, with the ambulance and transports in the middle. As they pulled away from the professor's house.

The sky began to get darker and darker, and the wind was beginning to howl.

As they passed through one empty town after another, Raghav wondered where everyone was. These places were familiar to him, stops on his frequent drives to Amritsar. But they seemed like ghost towns — empty dhabas, tuck stops and hotels lining the roads, with not a single person or car travelling the highway. As though millions of people have disappeared overnight.

The pain in his shoulder was making him woozy, and from the wetness of the bandage, Raghav knew he was bleeding again. To ignore the pain, he closed his eyes and leaned against the canvas wall of the truck, trying to lose himself in the rhythmic rattling of the truck's movement.

Perhaps he'd fallen asleep for some time — he couldn't remember — Raghav opened his eyes, noticing that the rattling of the truck had come to an end.

The truck was bathed in darkness, and no one was making a sound—all, even the soldiers, were staring white-eyed through the broad windscreen in the front.

The sky was dark, and the wind was a howling gale of grey dust and mud. Lightning was forking through the air, though there was no thunder to be heard. And a rhythmic thumping—like the footsteps of God—could be heard.

And far in the distance, approaching the convoy from out of the grey fog, was a blurred white shape. The thumping was coming from the shape in the fog, getting sharper and louder as it got closer and closer. 'Strange,' thought Raghav worriedly, his eyes also fastened on the white figure in the fog. 'Sounds almost like hoofbeats.'

And then the white figure broke through the fog, and came to a halt about a hundred metres ahead of the convoy.

The sudden gasp that escaped Raghav's mouth—repeated by all in the truck—was the only sound in the sudden stillness.

The white figure was a horse, a towering, enormous beast, easily bigger than the army transport they rode in. Its mane and tail seemed to be of white fire, and a dark figure, shaped like a man, sat across its back.

But no man was ever that tall—easily ten feet or more, dressed in a glowing, pale robe that seemed to radiate power. Its features could not be seen at this distance, except for two bright, glowing spots of light were its eyes would have been. And a third spot, also glowing, just above them.

The figure raised an enormous hand.

The world went black.

...